Five Little Piggies

This little piggy went to market.
This little piggy stayed home.
This little piggy had roast beef.
This little piggy had none
And this little piggy cried,
"Wee wee wee," all the
way home!

If that's all you've ever
been told about the five little
piggies, you may wonder
what the *real* story is. *Why*
did one piggy go to market,
whereas another stayed
home? And *what* could
have sent the littlest piggy
running toward home at
such a clip?

Now David Martin spills
the whole hoggy truth in
five little stories, each
hilariously illustrated by
Susan Meddaugh, creator
of *Martha Speaks, Martha
Calling,* and other
popular picture
books.

To my brother, Ben
D. M.

For John F.
S. M.

ISBN 0-439-07720-6

Text copyright © 1998 by David Martin. Illustrations copyright © 1998 by Susan Meddaugh. All rights reserved. Published by Scholastic Inc., 555 Broadway, New York, NY 10012, by arrangement with Candlewick Press. SCHOLASTIC and associated logos are trademarks and/or registered trademarks of Scholastic Inc.

12 11 10 9 8 7 6 5 4 3 2 1   8 9/9 0 1 2 3/0

Printed in the U.S.A.   14

First Scholastic printing, October 1998

This book was typeset in Stone Informal.
The pictures were done in watercolor and ink.

Five Little Piggies

Yoo-hoo!
Little
Piggies!

stories by David Martin

illustrated by Susan Meddaugh

Scholastic Inc.
New York Toronto London Auckland Sydney
Mexico City New Delhi Hong Kong

This Little Piggy
Went to Market

"Little Piggy, will you go to market? We need eggs and milk and apples," said Momma Piggy.

"Sure," said Little Piggy. And she went to market singing,

♫ Eggs and milk and apples.
Megs and milk and mapples.
Pegs and pilk and papples.

When she got to the market she said,

On the way home she saw some chickens and cows eating apples.

"Oh, now I remember!" said Little Piggy, and she ran back to market and bought eggs and milk and apples.

"Mommy, I'm back," said Little Piggy.

"Good. Did you get everything?" said Momma Piggy.

"Oh, they're delicious pooples," said Momma Piggy.
"And here's a great big **BUG** for my silly piggy wiggy."

② This Little Piggy Stayed Home

SPLASH!

Little Piggy spilled his juice.

CRASH!

He dropped his cereal on the floor.

RIP!

His pants split and all the other little piggies laughed at him.

Momma Piggy said, "I think you should stay home with me today." And she sent the others off to school.

All day long Little Piggy and Momma Piggy cooked and ate and played together.

"We had slopcakes and syrup for lunch!" said Little Piggy when the others came home from school.

The next day, all the other little piggies spilled their milk and dropped their cereal on the floor.

"Mommy, today can we stay home with you?" they asked.
"Of course you can," said Momma Piggy.

"Not me," said Little Piggy.
"I'm going to school."

3

This Little Piggy Had Roast Beef

"Little piggies, come and eat," called Momma Piggy.

"Not slops again!" said Little Piggy. "Why can't we have roast beef?"

"Okay," said Momma Piggy. "Here's some roast beef."

"It's good, but something is missing," said Little Piggy.

"Try it with some potatoes," said Momma Piggy.

"It still isn't right," said Little Piggy.

"Here, dump in these bananas your brother sat on," said Momma Piggy.

"Oh, that's good," said Little Piggy. "Can we put in the rotten eggs from breakfast, too?"

"Yummy!" said Little Piggy, and she threw in last week's soup and a squishy pickle.

"Now it's perfect. Try some, Momma!"

"Delicious!" said Momma Piggy.
"But it tastes like slops to me."
"No," said Little Piggy.
"That's not slops. That's

ROAST BEEF!"

4

This Little Piggy Had None

One day Momma Piggy went shopping and came home with treats for everyone.

But Little Piggy
dropped his
ice cream

and his
balloons
flew away

and then Little Piggy
had none.

Little Piggy cried and cried.

MOMMY!
I want
ice Cream!
I want
balloons!

Suddenly the other little piggies began to cry, too. And they cried even harder.

"Uh, oh. You four piggies all have chickenpox," said Momma Piggy. "But not you, Little Piggy. You have no spots, NONE!"

"Mommy! I **WANT** spots!" said Little Piggy.
"Okay," said Momma Piggy. "You can have spots, too."

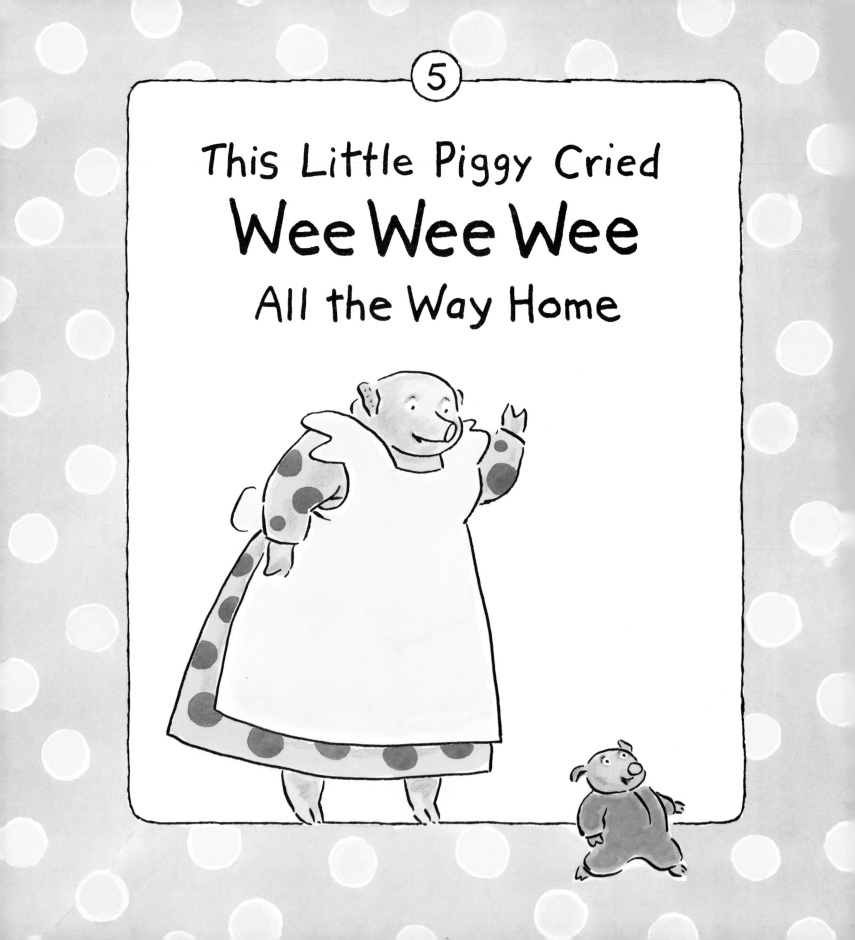

5

This Little Piggy Cried
Wee Wee Wee
All the Way Home

Little Piggy was playing with the piggies next door.

Suddenly she got up and started running.
"Wee wee wee," she cried.

"What's the matter, Little Piggy?" asked her sister.

"Why are you crying?" asked her brother.

"Did you hurt yourself, Little Piggy?" asked Momma Piggy.
But Little Piggy just ran faster and cried,
"Wee wee wee," all the way home.

Then she cried,
"Wee
wee
wee,"
all the
way up
the stairs.

And she cried, "Wee wee wee," all the way to the bathroom.

"*OH!*" said Little Piggy when she came out. "That felt good. I really had to go!"